HIGH-WIRE HENRY

by Mary Calhoun ★ illustrated by Erick Ingraham

Morrow Junior Books
New York

To my youngest grandson, Sean, with love   M.C.

Text copyright © 1991 by Mary Calhoun
Illustrations copyright © 1991 by Erick Ingraham

Inquiries should be addressed to
William Morrow and Company, Inc.,
105 Madison Avenue, New York, NY 10016.

Printed in the United States of America.
1   2   3   4   5   6   7   8   9   10

Library of Congress Cataloging-in-Publication Data

Calhoun, Mary.
    High-wire Henry / by Mary Calhoun ; illustrated by Erick Ingraham.
        p.   cm.
    Summary: Although Henry the cat learns tightrope walking only to
impress the humans in his family, who have stopped paying attention
to him because of their new puppy, his skill comes in handy when the
puppy gets stranded on a high ledge.
    ISBN 0-688-08983-6.—ISBN 0-688-08984-4 (lib. bdg.)
    [1. Cats—Fiction. 2. Dogs—Fiction. 3. Tightrope walking—
Fiction.]   I. Ingraham, Erick, ill. II. Title.
PZ7.C1278Hk   1991
[E]—dc20   89-35642   CIP   AC

*The full color artwork was
prepared using pencil and watercolor.
The book was set in 18 point ITC
Garamond Light.*

When The Man brought a puppy in, Henry went out…

and stayed out. That night he climbed the apple
tree and crouched on a branch. Huffing his fur
against a drizzle of rain, he looked through
the window.

Inside, the puppy played while they all watched—The Kid, The Woman, and The Man. The puppy caught a Ping-Pong ball in his mouth, spurted it out, and pounced after it.

"Isn't that cute!" exclaimed The Man. "He's cute as a button."

"What shall we call him?" asked The Woman.

"I know!" The Kid said. "Let's call him Buttons."

"Mow," Henry moaned. For all he cared, they could call that pup Rosebud.

Next morning the puppy saw him in the tree and jumped at the trunk. "Yap, yap!"

"Poor cat, he can't get down," The Woman said.

Poor cat, indeed! He was a hind-leg walker, some smart cat. To remind them, Henry stood up and stepped along the branch.

"Wow!" cried The Kid. "Henry's like a high-wire walker!" Henry sashayed along the branch, switching his tail.

"Henry, we know you're wonderful," The Woman said. "Now please come down."

Henry did. And it wasn't his fault, when he backed down the trunk, that Buttons jumped up and got a hind-claw scratch on his nose. "Yeef!"

The next day Henry watched The Man teach Buttons to do tricks. When the puppy rolled over on the grass—"Good dog!"—Henry sniffed. He could do *that*. In a spot of warm dust, he rolled over and over just for the feel on his fur. But he wouldn't roll over if someone asked him to!

The Man put a harness and leash on the puppy
to teach him to walk by his right foot. "Heel!"
Henry walked behind them on his back legs. Let
The Man praise *him* for how cleverly he walked.

Buttons saw the tall, standing-up cat. "Warf!" he said in astonishment. He jumped on his hind legs to lick Henry's face, and they both fell over. The Man laughed.

"Snaaa!" Henry ran away. He hated to be laughed at.

"Silly cat!" The Man called. "Buttons was only trying to make friends."

Silly cat, indeed! He would show that Man what a really smart animal could do. He'd be Henry the High-Wire Walker!

That night Henry practiced on the back fence. Rising to his back legs, he took one step, two steps.... This was better than trying to run on four feet along the rail.

Then he wobbled. Batting his paws didn't help,
so he waved his tail to catch his balance and
stretched his whiskers wide. In the dark, he could
feel the fence rail guiding his feet.

And it felt good! Henry had learned hind-leg walking by dancing to music on the stereo. To the tune of circus music he'd heard, Henry sang, "Yow yowie meowl! Me-e-yowul me-yowul meow."

From the house, The Man shouted, "Stop that caterwauling!"

The shout startled Henry. Falling, he caught the fence top with his front claws and scrambled back up. Never mind. Tomorrow he'd show that Man.

In the morning, while The Man, The Woman, and The Kid ate breakfast, Henry walked the clothesline, which was strung between two trees. Henry climbed a tree and stepped on the line.

The line was a twisted cord, thinner than the fence rail. And it didn't hold still like the fence. Henry curled his toes around the cord and stepped out.

He was walking in the air! Waving his tail, Henry hummed a purr and burst into song. "Yow yowie meowl!"

The Kid saw him. "Look at Henry! He's walking the clothesline!"

"What in the world?" cried The Man.

But the line swayed too much. Henry teetered, and whipped his tail to catch his balance. No use. He was falling. Henry fell.

Of course, he landed on his feet, and the grass
was soft. But the *whump* shook his eyeballs.

They all ran out. "Henry, are you hurt?" "Oh
dear!" "Yap yap!" "What possessed the cat?" That
was The Man.

How embarrassing! Henry sat with his back to
them, lashing his tail. The puppy ran to lick him,
and Henry hissed.

"Leave him alone." The Kid pulled Buttons away and smoothed Henry's head. "You're a great high-wire walker! You just need to carry a balancing rod."

Henry crouched away from The Kid's hand. Trying to show off, he'd made a fool of himself. Cats don't do tricks!

After that, he sat in the apple tree a lot.
The Man would never like a cat.

One day he saw a squirrel run across the telephone wire to the house and hop to a ledge under the upper windows. One window was open. Would that snoopy squirrel go in?

Instead—"Yap yap!"—Buttons popped out the window and scampered along the ledge after the squirrel.

"Yowl!" Henry stood up in the tree. The ledge was narrow. Let him fall, Henry thought. But—no. He didn't want the foolish dog to get hurt.

Henry rushed down the tree. "Yow-meowl!" he yelled. *Help!* Where was everybody?

The squirrel turned the corner of the house,
but the puppy stopped and looked down. "Yeef!"
he cried. He tried to turn around, but he couldn't.
"Yeef yeef!"

"Yow-meowl!" Henry called. The door to the
house was closed. How would he get up there?
The same way the squirrel did. Henry raced to the
telephone pole by the back fence.

But—he hadn't been able to walk the clothesline without falling. He needed a balancing rod.

Seizing a stick in his teeth, Henry sprang up the
pole. His claws slipped on the smooth wood, not
like tree bark. But he thought *up, up*—and
scrabbled up the pole because he knew he could.

He put out one paw–then another. The wire
was even thinner and more slippery than the
clothesline. "Mow," Henry moaned.
"Yeef yeef!" Buttons wailed.

So Henry stood up and clutched the stick with his front paws. And it made a good balance, like having longer whiskers!

Henry skated his feet along the wire, step, step, *steady, steady.*

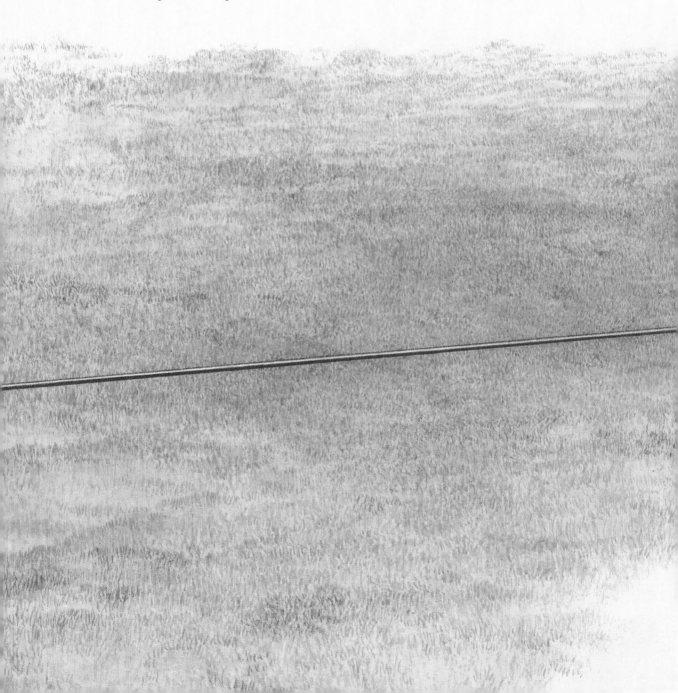

When the wire swayed, he swayed with it,
waving the stick and his tail. He was doing it! He
was high-wire walking! And nobody there to see it.

Then The Kid and The Man came out of the house, and The Kid saw him. "Henry!"
"Yeeeef!" Buttons cried.

"Good grief!" The Man exclaimed. "Be careful,
Henry! Hang on to him! I'll get the ladder!"
One more step and Henry was on the ledge.

Dropping the stick, he ran to Buttons and shouldered him against the house. Hang on to him? How? Henry gripped the dog's collar in his teeth.

"Hold on!" The Man set the ladder next to them.

Buttons shivered and yelped. If he panicked, they'd both fall over the edge. "Purr," Henry hummed to soothe the puppy.

And there came The Man up the ladder. "Good cat!" he said. He put the puppy under one arm. "Stupid dog!" He climbed down with Buttons.

"Yay for Henry the Hero!" The Kid shouted.

"Yowl!" Henry pranced at the praise. Except—
he looked down at The Man patting the puppy.

Henry crouched by the ladder. "Mew," he said
in a small voice. He couldn't climb down a ladder.

The Man grinned up at him. "You old rascal!
You could go in the way Buttons came out.
However"—The Man climbed the ladder and
took Henry on his shoulder—"you deserve a ride."

"Yow-meowl!" proclaimed Henry, riding The Man's shoulder. He was some smart cat!

C